Twisted Tales 2016

First Published by

RAGING AARDVARK PUBLISHING, Dalveen, Australia

http://ragingaardvark.com

Cover Image and Design by A Mitchell

ISBN-10: 0-9945252-0-6
ISBN-13: 978-0-9945252-0-8
All rights reserved.

Twisted Tales 2016

Twisted

Tales

Flash Fiction with a Twist

2016

Edited by Annie Evett and

Margie Riley

Raging Aardvark Publishing

Twisted Tales

showcases

the winners of one of the

competitions held celebrating

(Inter)National Flash Fiction Day 2016

Preface

Each year, I am gratified to see flash fiction become more mainstream and accepted as a genre in its own right. Flash fiction writers share a small but intimate space, where—although characters don't have the opportunity to fully develop—integral writing elements must still be upheld.

Flash fiction is about tight structure, vivid images and focus. The critical skill in writing flash fiction is the ability to convey the message with brevity. There simply isn't the time to entice the reader with atmospheric detail. Sentences need to be fast-paced and focused.

The best flash fiction is a complete parcel within its restricted word count. A perfect opening sentence isn't enough to sway readers or judges. The endings of these stories needed to leave a question, give a chill or force the reader to read the piece again to pick up the clues they had glossed over. Within a short time, the writers need to get inside the reader's head, have an intellectual and emotional impact. And stop.

Our entrants' stories this year were filled with characters leaping out of the page demanding attention. Some will make you shiver, others give pause for you to reminisce and pull heart strings—but all will leave an impression.

I hope that you enjoy these stories every bit as much as the judges and editors have.

Contents

Acknowledgements

What a job! How difficult was it for our judges to choose a dozen tales from the collection of high quality stories they were presented with...

I am struck with gratitude annually and feel it is an incredible honour to read the submissions from around the globe for the year's competition. The support and encouragement received every year fuels our passion to continue and we would like to thank all those involved with the Twisted Tales project.

It was wonderful to include established writers beside emerging authors within this anthology, and heartwarming to receive messages from thrilled contributors excited to launch their careers.

To the year's judges who are short story writers and experienced wordsmiths, a huge thank you for your insights, guidance and dedication to uphold quality.

Once again an enormous debt of gratitude to Margie Riley for her editing and proofreading skills, her late night conversations and constant encouragement.

Thank you to the wonderful readers within our networks, for your added assistance and enthusiasm in the "People's Choice" selection process.

Without the support and encouragement of Calum Kerr, Director of (Inter)National Flash Fiction Day, this collection would not have reached the audiences and garnered the interest it has.

Most importantly, I'd like to thank family and close friends for their ongoing support and encouragement. *Twisted Tales*, and all of the creations within Raging Aardvark Publishing, truly would not happen without them.

Annie Evett

Publisher

Margie's Red Pen

When Annie asked me to help with the editing of *Twisted Tales,* what could I say? I love to read, love to write and love to edit. *Quid pro quo!* I get to read and edit and Annie gets late night chats.

I don't mind those either. Thank you, Annie, for the opportunity to contribute—just a little—again.

Mystery Mail

by Jodie How

I shove the pile of edge-worn letters I've collected over the past five years under the covers of my standard issue bed.

Last Friday, I received the latest letter in the post. It's from a Ms Fueng. I've kept it in my pocket all week, rereading it several times a day. This is another clue to the puzzle I feel compelled to solve, for the sake of my sanity.

She says she needs to meet with me. She says it's important; urgent. She says she has to visit soon, or it'll be too late. Apparently, he is dying.

I don't know her. She has no right to demand anything of me. I won't be obliging her. Or him.

He is running for President. He is Zane Blackwood—political mastermind. Womaniser. Not your all-round, Regular Bastard. No. Evil Narcissist-Bastard.

Aisha says I'm taking this letter too seriously. Aisha says not to worry about it. Aisha says I ought to be spending my time concentrating on more important things, like getting better.

Zane Blackwood. The man who chained me, naked, to a banister in his apartment and left me there for three days, alone. The man who makes my skin crawl with fear.

I have no doubt that he put her up to writing this letter to me. He is playing her like a fiddle. He will go to any expense to draw me out, expose me, make me utterly vulnerable—to strike, damage, destroy.

They don't know where I am. They can't know for sure that the letter has reached me. They make their moves based on educated guesswork.

I'm not worried. I've kept myself hidden for five years now. I don't doubt my expert skills in deception. I've always been a few steps ahead of him.

Meeting is no use. Meeting won't help me. Meeting is something I can't do—not after the progress I've made in the last five years. I'd rather live with the mystery of her letter than go seeking the truth.

No. I need to remain anonymous. I need to keep the past in the past. I need to remind myself to forget about him and keep moving forward.

I write: "Return to Sender" on the face of the envelope. I write: "Not at this Address" next to that. Then I reseal the envelope securely—Ms Fueng's letter inside. Then I put the envelope on the communal pile of mail ready to post, noting the flamboyance of my capital letters.

I wash my hands with antiseptic soap for exactly twenty-five seconds—five seconds longer than recommended by infectious disease specialists—just to be sure. I stare at myself in the mirror. I still don't recognise the face staring back at me. They tell me that's Carrie.

I take the little purple pill from Aisha's plastic medicine cup. The nurse watches me swallow the medication and chase it down with a few chugs of water.

I pause and think again, staring at my bed and thumbing the hem of my gown.

Each letter came from a different woman (he never wrote) but each letter was really a message from him.

The ink on each letter should look different. The writing style of each letter should be different.

All the letters are written in the same, cursive

handwriting, in the same ink. Why do they all look exactly the same? All capital letters are printed with a flourish.

I feel it's a mystery I repeatedly get so close to solving but never quite nail.

Norfolk Beach.

Original Photograph

by Christopher Stanley

Norfolk

by Christopher Stanley

We arrive at the bungalow after midnight, Eddie snoring in his booster seat and Happisburgh lighthouse winking in the distance. It's exactly as I remember it from my childhood, with waves crunching beyond the dunes and the salty tang of the sea breeze. This is it, I think, as I unpack my travel-weary limbs from the car. Eccles-on-Sea, on the North Norfolk coast, is where I'm going to find the horror story that resurrects my career.

I'm supposed to be an author but I haven't sold a book in half a decade, not since my wife, Rosemary, gave birth to a boy-flavoured bundle of toothless smiles and Godless nappies. Eddie wasn't planned and it's hard not to blame him for my aborted career. The only reason I brought him with me is because Rosemary insisted I learn to write with him in the room. I tried to argue, pleading the need for authorial solitude, but he's here and she's not.

Half of Eccles was stolen by the sea some centuries ago and what's left is barely a ghost town. They say a storm once shifted so much sand from the beach it uncovered the old graveyard, tearing open coffins and scattering skeletons up the coast. "With history like that," said Rosemary, "who needs horror?"

I fall asleep listening to the wind tugging at the dunes. In my dreams, the spirits of the dead crawl from the water to steal Eddie away, their fleshless fingers prising him from my grasp. I'm glad they're taking him but I'm compelled to ask why. One word comes hissing back: "Innocent."

I'm startled into consciousness by something clawing at my face. When I switch on the bedside light,

Eddie's on top of me, saying he had a nightmare in which hollow-eyed ghosts crossed the dunes and descended on our bungalow. "They took me away from you," he whispers, unaware of how similar our dreams were.

Outside, the shed creaks in the wind while rain pelts the windows. And there's something else, something more deliberate. I hold Eddie tight, telling him there are no ghosts, only stories, but something is thumping the walls of the bungalow. The look on Eddie's face says it all. The spirits have come for him; our dreams are coming true.

"I'll try not to let them get you, Eddie."

"You have to!"

For a moment, I'm confused, but then I remember that Eddie woke me up mid-dream. "In your nightmare," I say, "where did the ghosts take you?"

"To the safe place."

It isn't rain hitting the windows; it's spray from the rising sea. And the thumping sound is water. Somewhere in the bungalow a window shatters, and then another. The two halves of Eccles are going to be reunited, tonight. I cling desperately to Eddie, promising him I'll never let go.

"I'll really miss you, Daddy," he says, pushing me away. "But I'll tell everyone what happened and I'm sure they'll buy your books again."

Retail Therapy

by Keith Gillison

"So, I went to the shop to get food for my tarantula and came home with food for my tarantula—and an Asian jungle scorpion," Helen said, from her comfortable position lying on the leather sofa.

Dr. Miller nodded and gestured for her to continue.

"She's called Nyx, after the Greek goddess of the night. All my invertebrates are named after Greek goddesses."

"And how did your husband react to this?" asked Miller.

Helen frowned.

"Not too well. He"s unhappy about me turning the spare room into a tropical arachnid and reptile house.

We had another row."

"Because of the tarantulas?"

"It's an Asian jungle scorpion, and no it wasn't because of that." Helen sat upright on the sofa. "I bought some other items while I was out."

"Aha," said Miller. He placed his reading glasses on and sat poised with pen and notebook. "And what did you buy?"

Helen scrunched her face in thought.

"I was on such a high from the Asian jungle scorpion purchase that I felt like rewarding myself, so I popped to M&S and bought this lovely black dress. It's gorgeous, reduced to £200. They were practically giving it away."

Dr. Miller sighed and shook his head. He adjusted his spectacles as he made notes. It was something he'd seen therapists do in movies.

"After I got the dress I was buzzing so I treated myself to some new heels."

"And how did that make you feel?" Miller may have only been practising psychotherapy for a few years since graduation, but he was a firm believer in the maxim "if in doubt, ask a question."

"Amazing! I felt fantastic," Helen beamed as she fidgeted with her hands. "So I popped to the jewellery counter and got myself a pair of silver earrings and a pearl necklace and then..."

Dr. Miller scribbled frantically on the pad. He couldn't keep up with his patient.

"I bought a bottle of perfume," Helen panted. "Wait, it was two bottles." She jumped to her feet.

Dr Miller stopped writing. He recognised the signs.

"OK, I think you need to try and calm down. Can you

sit down please and we'll practice your breathing exercises."

"Oh sod that! I feel incredible. I could just do with nipping to the shops now; get some crickets for the scorpion, a mouse for the snake and then pop into Next —they've got a sale on."

Dr. Miller placed his hands on Helen's shoulders.

"Breathe with me now, in...and out...in..."

"I don't want to," Helen yelled, pushing him away. "I want to go shopping. The thought of all those shops— God it turns me on so much. I feel like running out, grabbing the nearest man and..."

"Whoa! Stop there, please. I've been through this with you before; we're here to talk about your shopping problem. If you need a sex therapist I can recommend some very good ones."

"Huh," Helen snapped. "You're such a prude. Every time I talk about sex you try and get rid of me. Shopping turns me on, you can't ignore that."

"No, no," Miller bleated. "I'm not going there. I think it's best you see another therapist."

Helen jumped in front of the door, blocking Miller's attempt to usher her out.

"You ungrateful... Your practice would be tiny if it wasn't for me sending all my mad friends here. And what thanks do I get? Well, I want to talk about sex. Why won't you let me? Why?"

Miller blushed and took a deep breath.

"Because I only agreed to these stupid sessions to stop Dad going bankrupt over your crazy spending, that's why. If you carry on like this you'll lose the house, Mum, and you're not bloody well living with me!"

Helen Miller shrugged and looked at the floor.

"I suppose I could take the scorpion back."

A Yellow Star

by Sylvia Petter

Gertrude pulled on her precious pair of silk stockings, checked to see that the seams ran straight and tied a shoelace just under the knee to keep them up. The hem of her blue floral cotton dress dipped just below the knee to cover any unsightliness. She pinched her cheeks to make them blush red, dipped a moist finger into a little pot of rouge and dabbed it gently on her lips. She pinned her shoulder-length curly hair behind her ears, smiled at the old mirror with its brown stains, and tucked her white clutch bag under one arm. He was coming. She had to go. She had to be in the front row. She had to be where he could see her.

Down on the street, people were already milling towards the square. He had promised a gift to women born the same day as he. She shared his birthday. How would he know? Her birthday was a month later when the daffodils would be in bloom. She could always write to him. Tell him. Wish him happy birthday. Somehow link herself to him that way. Just noticing her in the crowd, bestowing a smile, a gaze on her, would really be gift enough, she thought.

She pushed her way through the crowd—*Verzeihung: Pardon*—and was soon at the corner of the street where the cavalcade must pass. His car would have to turn. The sun shone high in the sky. It was a fine day. He would be standing in an open car. He would see her. He had to see her.

An open car followed by two black limousines and six motorbikes moved slowly towards the corner where Gertrude stood. The cavalcade slowed down to turn and the man in the open car stood, saluted with a stretched out arm, and let his gaze caress the rows of upturned faces. He raised his head and looked out towards the throng, some stretching to see all the more of him.

Gertrude, her back against the wall of the corner building stood on her tiptoes. He was looking straight at her. The colour rushed from her neck to her cheeks, her eyes sparkled. He had seen her. Then she went white. The man frowned then tossed his head and looked away. Gertrude felt her heart thump. People turned towards her. They were coming at her. She could not escape.

The next day the papers reported that a young woman had been crushed to death. An accident. The young boy with the yellow star had had no right to be there. The police made only one arrest.

Previously published at Folded Word, 2015

Pumpkin

by Jon Stubbington

Mother took a firm hold of her largest knife, steadied herself against the kitchen table and, with a grunt, sliced the top off completely. The Eldest caught the top as it slid off, falling forward towards the floor.

"There you go. Get your hands in and scoop out the insides."

She placed it on the table in front of them. The Youngest had to stand on a chair to reach up and over and inside, grabbing handfuls and dropping them onto the table top. Mother pulled a plate from the cupboard and set it down next to them.

"Make sure that you keep it all; we shall make it into a pie."

Youngest continued to scoop out the insides, leaning further and further across the table as her little hands delved deeper into the cavity she was creating. Eldest gathered up what they had already pulled out and dropped it onto the large white plate on the table.

Looking up from her task Youngest said, "Mother, there are some bits I cannot get out."

Mother searched in a drawer until she found a smaller knife. "Watch out Youngest, this knife is sharp. Let me see if I cannot free the last pieces for you." She worked the knife around the inside, separating any remaining strands until the whole of the inside was free to be scooped up and out and onto the plate. "Well done children; we shall make a particularly delicious pie for Father's dinner."

The small knife was handed to Eldest with the instructions that he was not to harm himself on the sharp blade.

"Would you like to cut out the eyes?" asked Mother.

With the relish of a young boy, Eldest set to work in carving out the eyes. He worked away with the little blade until there were two dark holes either side of the nose. "Will that do Mother?" he asked in hope that he had completed the task well.

"The one on the left is smaller," said Youngest, holding her head on one side and giving a critical appraisal of her brother's work.

"It's just fine as it is," Mother reassured him. "Now what about the mouth? I think he would like a nice big smile."

Eldest gave a smile himself as he set to work, slicing up and around, lengthening out the mouth so that the ends curled up into a great grin. He cut nicks into the lips so that he could pull the skin back, with teeth to poke through underneath.

Youngest shuddered. "That's horrible," she said, the delight dripping from her words. "We should give him a name."

"He already has a name," explained Mother. "He is called Jack and once upon a time he made a deal with the devil. He made the devil promise that he would never take his soul. But when Jack died, he could go not to heaven—for he had not led a good life—nor would the devil take him to hell, so he was forced to roam the world with only an eternal flame from the underworld to light his way."

Mother struck a match to light a candle, which she placed carefully inside the hollowed head.

Eldest laid down the knife next to the plate holding the scooped-out insides. He considered the head staring up at him from the table, with its empty eyes and clownish smile.

"But that's a silly story Mother," he said at last.

"Why is that Eldest?" asked Mother.

"Because when he died he didn't wander alone with only a light to guide him. When he died he came home with us." He picked up a jumper from the floor and read the name from the badge pinned to the front. "And his name isn't Jack; it's Brian."

Mother smiled at him and wrapped her arm around his shoulders. "Well, it's only a story. It doesn't have to make sense."

Youngest joined them in their hug. "Next year Mother," she asked, "can we have a pumpkin instead?"

Plasma Rifle Etiquette

by Heather Harris McFarlane

I wanted to go to a lecture at the university. I've never really thought of myself as an especially smart guy, but I like to learn new stuff, you know? I thought it'd be pretty cool to see what it was like in school on the alien moon, test out how well I'd picked up the language and all that. If I'd just gone and done that, I might not be sitting here, waiting to hear if my life's over from some guy whose title is 'Agent.' My friend Tsuki was determined to go and see the big solar array, though, and she's the one who paid attention in all the cultural sensitivity seminars and got me to apply for the trip in the first place, so I figured, whatever. It's cool. We'll go. We'll look at it. We'll write a paper about it.

So, we went, and man, it put any military bases I've seen to shame. You know those guards in London—the ones that aren't even allowed to smile? It's like that, but so many of them. You can't breathe without bumping into one, and then there's more walking around, aiming these big-ass rifles around. There was some engineer who gave a presentation about the solar array and how it worked and what it did, but I was too jumpy to pay attention. I'd noticed a button had fallen off my backpack, because of course it did, and after all those lectures about how to represent our planet and the excessively harsh penalties for any infractions, I figured I couldn't just leave it there. Plus, it was a Captain Marvel button, and Earth's Mightiest Hero just might be a clue that it was one of us who'd littered. I tried to be smooth about it, but I could feel the sweat making my shirt stick to me while I sort of just drifted back through the group 'til I could reach the damn thing. I knew it was just a matter of time before someone figured out I was the screw-up.

Sure enough, I got to the edge of the crowd, and as soon as I went to take one step out of bounds, I turned around and suddenly I'm nose-to-nose with whatever bayonet thing was on the end of this guy's gun. I screamed. You're damn right, I screamed. You would too if you saw that thing coming at your face. Damn near peed my pants.

That got some attention, and before I knew it, there were more guns, and more people yelling, and not only was I a disgrace to my planet, but I was gonna be in jail, too. I was freaking out, but the guy whose gun was in my face—he just cracked up! Laughed his ass off. I guess I was in shock, 'cause all of a sudden, all I could think was, damn, that is a great laugh. Pretty great rest of him, too, if I'm being honest. I can't help it; I have a type. I like a guy who's built enough to go rock climbing or surf with me, and well, he was definitely that.

Come to find out it was his first day, and he was nervous after getting all these lectures on dealing with the Earth people, so he had just as much explaining to do as I did. Just as well I liked the look of him, 'cause we both spent the rest of the day telling all the people in charge of both our groups all the details about how nothing had actually happened. Sitting through all that, we got to know each other a little, and turns out he wasn't just good-looking; he was funny, too. He'd picked up enough English to not need a translator, and if I wasn't in the biggest trouble I'd ever been in in my whole life, I'd have been cracking up. Bless his heart, he kept trying, though, while I just kept freaking out. We swapped contact info, just in case there was any follow-up to the incident, and, well, here I am—sitting in yet another bright, freezing cold government waiting room, surrounded by more big dudes with big guns, about to lose my damn mind. And this time, I don't have a hot guy to tell me dumb-ass jokes to get me through it. So, thanks. Once this agent approves his visa, you come and dance at our wedding?

Dedicated to the 49 precious lives lost at Pulse nightclub in Orlando, Florida on June 12, 2016.

Amor vincit omnia.

Boxed In

by Emily Forster

She looked down at the box she was holding, and hesitated. It had been overfilled. The walls bulged outwards and she could feel the flimsy cardboard warping around her fingers, unable to support the weight. Her shift was over. She should put down the box.

There is a kind of exhaustion where you are so tired that sleep becomes impossible. Heavy with fatigue, your body sinks into the mattress, desperate for unconsciousness, but your brain refuses to cooperate. It skitters from one random thought to another, directionless and unstoppable. Like shadows in candlelight, all the little things you have to forget just to get through the day flare up to monstrous proportions.

You try to clear your mind, concentrate on breathing, count sheep, but the torrent of thoughts flows on, relentless, exhausting. The tick tock of the clock chisels away the minutes. Five hours until morning. Four. Three. And if you do—miraculously—succeed in dropping off, the alarm intrudes all too quickly.

There was a small tear in the top left-hand corner furthest from her body. She watched it creep inexorably downwards. She imagined she could feel the fibres stretching, straining to cling together until the last possible moment as they were wrenched apart. It was going to split. She should put it down.

The day after a sleepless night is like a hangover. With an aching head, sore eyes, dry mouth and jittery stomach, you force yourself out of bed. You pray that the shower will wake you up. Peering bleary-eyed into the mirror you recoil from the apparition gawping back at you. Splash red eyes with cold water. Smear make-up onto grey-tinged skin. Try to humanise the zombie in the reflection.

She thought her arms must ache, but she couldn't feel it. Her fingertips were white where they gripped the cardboard. She stood motionless, expressionless, watching the slow progress of the fissure as it lengthened and gaped. She should put down the box.

When starved of sleep, emotions are thrown into sharp relief. Minor setbacks become catastrophes. Negative thoughts clamour for attention. The unfairness of working long hours for pitiful wages, at a place where pay is docked for the slightest reason and employment is never guaranteed more than a week ahead. Where the Head Manager monitors your every move and can terminate your contract in an instant. Where you can never make friends because the turnover is so fast and chatting is a sacking offence. Where exhaustion and depression join forces to prevent you from ever escaping this hell.

She should have put it down. With sudden violence the cargo lurched towards the opening, forcing its cardboard walls apart in a bid for freedom. At that moment she was overcome by the strange phenomenon whereby excessive fatigue is converted to hyperactivity. The myriad little injustices crowded together in her mind. With a grim smile she hurled the box into the air. People dived for cover, screaming as plastic shrapnel rained down upon them. Roaring, she rampaged along the aisles, shaking the shelves until they toppled, contents cascading across the floor. Crushing anything in her path, she tore through the warehouse, destruction in her wake.

The office door loomed ahead. The home of her

oppressor. It was locked. She wrenched a fire extinguisher from the wall and attacked. There was a satisfying crunch of splintering wood. A second blow smashed the lock from the frame and the door swung inwards. There was the Head Manager. Alone. Exposed. Vulnerable. Spinning like a hammer thrower she propelled the extinguisher at her enemy. With a piercing battle cry she launched herself after it, fists whirling. This monster must be destroyed.

Pain flooded her arms and hands as the adrenaline wore off. On the verge of collapse, she mustered all her strength for one final, deadly blow. Her adversary fell to the ground, vanquished. Strong hands gripped her arms and dragged her out of the room through crowds of dumbstruck colleagues. Blood dripped from her bruised knuckles and she could hear the whine of police sirens, but she had triumphed.

'FATAL ERROR' flashed across a blue screen.

"Hey!" She started at the sound. "You won't get paid any overtime! Give me that and go home." She blinked at the shift supervisor, his hands outstretched.

She looked down at the box she was holding, and hesitated.

Children's Games

by Alyson Faye

I've lost track of how long they've been out there; waiting. I can't run any longer. My chest burns, the cuts on my legs and arms throb. One of them is infected I am sure. I just don't look at it anymore. There is no point.

"Horsey, horsey, don't you stop."

The voices whisper, cry out, taunt. From over there in those scrubby bushes, from high up on the wire fence, and from behind me. They are all around me. I can see black shapes flitting, like ravens. Only, ravens leave you alone.

"Come out, come out, wherever you are."

Laughter trickling, like waves undulating. The first stone hits my right cheek. I feel warmth as the blood trickles down. It's just another cut to add to the long list of my injuries. A Coke can lands at my feet, a bottle splinters over my shoulder smacking down on the concrete. I am in their playground.

I wrap my tatty mac around me, shiver and wish I had not come here this evening. I had been to all the usual spots, but I was too late and they had been occupied. I'd had a couple of nights in hospital last month when I'd cut myself so badly I'd passed out and someone had called an ambulance. Best two nights I'd had in ages they were too. Warm bed, clean sheets, food and drink. Bliss.

We all know the old schoolhouse and its yard are best avoided. But I'd run out of choices. I'd hoped they wouldn't be there that night. I had got it wrong.

"Ring a ring o' roses."

Their shadows leap and dance in a circle,

overlapping. Fluttering like scraps of paper.

"All fall down."

Screams of laughter. The shadows slip into the ground and slide away. I start to recite the only protection I can think of which I learnt as a child from my mother, long gone now. God rest her soul. She did her best.

"Our father who art in Heaven..."

Another missile hits me, a glancing blow. I shrug it off. Try and act tough. I want to make myself as small as possible so I curl up in a ball.

"Bloody little monsters," I whisper. "Go away!"

Each breath hurts. My teeth ache profoundly. My vision blurs then clears. I pray not to pass out. Not here, in this place.

"Jack be nimble, Jack be quick."

They are urging me on. They want me to play with them.

They are an amorphous mass approaching me. Slowly they take shape. Some are dressed in jeans, others in pinafores, some in nightdresses. The youngest is sucking a grubby thumb. She's just a toddler. Her nightgown is stained dark brown. As if she is smeared in rust. She seems so innocent. Their laughing fades away. Silence falls. They all watch me. Will I run? Or am I done?

"Run, rabbit, run."

They sing with such hope shining out of their faces. Their eyes glinting in the moonlight.

I shake my head. I smell the spark in the air, before I see it, crackling out from their midst. They all gasp and watch it snake its way towards me in my newspaper lined coat. The air is thick with smoke and glee. My prayers turn to ashes.

"Boys and girls come out to play..."

The voices fade away. The shapes retreat in to the schoolhouse. They slip through its boarded-up windows, past the signs reading: *Beware—Trespassers!*" and are swallowed up into its grimy innards. Their home for many years.

Coming Undone

by Epiphany Ferrell

The last thing Fritz expected to find among his luggage was a tongue. A tongue was a strange find, even for someone with multiple entanglements in the entertainment world. Fritz knew it right away for a tongue, partly because it had been packed on ice inside a plastic bag and so retained something of a normal appearance, and partly because it was pierced with a bright sterling silver ball and he knew at least three people with similar piercings.

The door to his hotel room was still open, the under-tipped bellboy evidently not feeling himself sufficiently recompensed to close it, so Fritz quickly strode to it and shut it. It seemed the right thing to do. After all, the tongue had belonged to someone, and leaving it out for casual passers-by to gawk at was disrespectful. And quite probably illegal.

Fritz knew he should call the police and, naturally, he was disinclined to do so. People who deal with the famous and their secrets are in the habit of keeping secrets, not in the habit of enmeshing themselves in tedious and often detrimental-to-fame interviews with skeptical and boorish police officers. He wondered if the tongue belonged to one of his clients. It was an unpleasant thought; perhaps it meant that someone had spoken out of turn, or perhaps it meant that he himself was being warned against talking. He was unaware of any plot out of the ordinary which would require such a drastic message at this time, and that in itself was troubling. Overlooking the obvious was not a habit that led to continued employment.

One thing that was obvious—the tongue couldn't

remain in his hotel room. He thought about flushing it down the toilet, but seemed to remember from some cop drama in which one of his clients guest starred that such a plan was not failsafe. Perhaps a drink would clear his head, maybe cheer him up he thought, and so thinking, plucked the tongue in its iced plastic bag from his Kenneth Cole suitcase and dropped it into his jacket's inner pocket. Rather than risk wandering the hot streets and having the ice melt, Fritz elected to find a bar near his hotel.

The bar across the street, let's call it the Brazen Monkey (though that was not its name) was reasonably dark and crowded, but not too crowded. Fritz spent money, a bit of money, buying drinks for several young ladies at the bar. He ordered by name the vodka for their cocktails, which made them think it was top shelf. It wasn't. He settled on two who seemed to have conceived a dislike for each other, and let the others fade to the sidelines. The strawberry blonde seemed the nicer of the two, but the one with the olive complexion seemed sharper.

He bought them both milky cocktails with chocolate syrup around the rim of the glass. As he favored first one, then the other, with his intense blue-eyed sincerity, he dropped his hand to his pocket now and then, working the bag open, sliding the tongue into his hand. As soon as he had it, without a pause, he slipped it into Strawberry's drink. He did it while he leaned close to her diamonded ear, her glittered collarbone, to tell her god she was beautiful but she talked too fucking much. He said it loudly enough for Olive to hear, and hearing, to laugh a wicked, sensual, conqueror's laugh.

Fritz checked his watch, dropped a name, said he'd be back, and slid out of the bar light to the street. He congratulated himself on his cleverness.

He hadn't discovered the eyeball in his other pocket, yet.

This story appeared previously in Corvus Review.

Mirror

by Catherine Russell

Sebastian had heard family stories about the relic in the attic for years. However, he had always been a curious but sensible child and never believed the rumors of what lay beyond the locked door. Spirits and ghosts had no place in his imagination.

Nevertheless, the large standing object covered by the thin azure sheet had been gathering dust in a disused recess of the attic for centuries, according to family legend. The grandparents of his grandparents had feared the item hidden beneath the heavenly blue, yet feared to let it go; the consequences of its guardianship falling into careless hands might be too great.

In all likelihood, his elders had created the stories to

keep meddlesome children from scavenging through old family heirlooms, though Sebastian discovered nothing else of interest except a few scraps of antique clothing and some worn furniture. The secret hidden beneath the sheet would be revealed as nothing more than an ordinary mirror from a garage sale. With luck though, it might be valuable as an antique.

He pulled the silk off in one smooth motion, coughing from the dust borne on the air like dandelion seeds. The cloud dispersed, and he gazed at the image of the mirrored-attic. The same wooden walls, crossbeams, old trunks, and debris of generations were reflected back. But the staring face was not his own. The features were similar, high cheekbones, large round eyes and full sensual lips, but there any resemblance ended. Its deep brown eyes stared back at him from within a pale, hairless face. It lifted thin, bare hands to cover its mouth before it ran, screaming from the room.

Sebastian himself stepped back, reeling from the shock, grabbing at his face, his head, his horns. He sighed in relief when he felt his tail swish around his shoulders. He was fine. Who was that then? Some demonic version of himself trapped in a mirror world? He wondered if the beast was dangerous. Should he destroy the cursed mirror and rid himself of whatever lurked inside?

In the corner of the mirror, the blue cover was barely visible near the doorway of the looking-glass room. The creature returned to stand before him and Sebastian took a step back. Then, overcome with pity for the poor, bald thing trapped on the other side, Sebastian placed a lone claw upon the glass. The monster's eyes widened in terror, and it struck the translucent partition with something long and hard.

The mirror shattered.

Sebastian's last thoughts cut as deeply as the shards of falling crystal. He felt himself break into a thousand pieces.

#

The man's sigh filled the room.

Grabbing a broom, he hastily swept the fragments of broken glass onto the discarded sheet, then wrapped them tightly in their sky-colored shroud and entombed them in the waste bin. He shoved the bin away with his foot, once more sending clouds of dust into the attic's stale air. Turning his back on all, he hastily closed the door and locked it behind him.

Later he could tell himself it had only been a dream.

The Light Below

by Paul Alex Gray

Mika once told me it can't snow when it's too cold. I can't help but try to sound out the notes of his voice as I stand behind the curtain, facing the street like some children's book monster ashamed of its name.

The streetlight's orange glow is broken and fractured by a million flakes. They spill and swirl, sometimes twisting and turning, rising for a moment and falling back on themselves.

I see shadows claw and reach up the driveway. It's deep with snow. Dad hasn't bothered to clear it.

I see Kaden and James drift closer.

I move to the door but before I go out I peer back up the stairs. This place is so much bigger and quieter now and I think it's crazy that I can't see in the dark. I hear noise from the back room and know someone's passed out in front of the TV again.

I slip out into the night.

The wind traces along the frozen branches. Kaden is rugged up well, a scarf drawn across his face. James just wears a hoodie and there is ice in his hair and the scruff of his almost-beard. He stares blankly but reaches one hand out for my arm.

We are going to the place behind the school where the tall pines tell winter it can go to hell. We march in silence, across icy cleared footpaths. Of all things, the only sounds above the wind are those of a stop sign, trembling and squeaking.

Kaden stands before the gym wall, reaching into his pocket and curses.

"Too icy," he says, louder than I think he should.

I stare at the faded tags he marked before on the bricks. There is a curving line, an S that cuts out just before one end. Or maybe some other letter, unformed or unfinished.

"Let's go to the swings," says Jamie.

There are rocks buried in the snow, but there was a time when they were blazing hot embers in dusty grass. We couldn't even sit on them. Mika poured some water on one for me, "To cool it off," he'd said but it had dried up almost right away and the rock was still too hot.

"Come on!"

Jamie sits on a swing, head half buried in his hoodie, arms curled up awkwardly. I think he's whispering to himself but it's too hard to hear what he's saying.

The sky is strangely bright tonight, the clouds glow orange. It looks all wrong and I get an awful feeling and I want to run and run and run but I know that there is only this place now. The sky feels heavy, arching and heaving, glaring at the light on the fallen snow.

"What do you think Mika is up to this weekend?" asks Kaden.

Neither of us answers.

The icy branches tell a crackling story and I will remember it forever. We're a past tale now, finished with dreams crushed up and broken, hopes bleeding in metal and glass.

Once there were four.

It's not what I expected. I guess I'd hoped for stars or endless white light or maybe nothing at all. Not this empty endlessness.

If anything it's snowing even more. It comes in great white sheets, spilling and tumbling toward us. They'll maybe cancel school tomorrow. I hope they don't. I'd like to see Mika again. I'd follow him in and out of classrooms, and throughout the day. I'd stand beside him as he drew and trace my fingers around the edges of his world.

I wish I hadn't come out tonight. But there's an aching in the night that summons us. The wind tugs and pulls and I'm not even sure what we're going to do now.

Caroom!

by E. W. Farnsworth

"Caroom!" Randy Morley shouted.

With his clear bag of recyclables, the boy roller-boarded across Baseline before the yellow light turned red.

He kicked up onto the pavement and stood tall while he sailed down to the mall scanning the area for bottles, cans and whatnot along the path.

On a good day Randy collected a hundred aluminium cans, netting him five dollars, but for him the money was not as important as the game. He had fierce competition, particularly from Sam the bone-thin rag picker and Caramia the raging torch-haired teen.

Ahead, pushing his overflowing shopping cart was

Sam, inching forward, his laser eyes focusing on the minutiae most mall denizens missed: the baseball card peeking out from a trash receptacle or the penny, its edge shining at the edge of the grass.

"Hey, Sam!" the roller-boarder cried in cheerful greeting.

The rag picker paid him no attention. He kneeled to pick up a few pearls from huge cracks in the sidewalk.

"Hey, Randy!" Caramia sang out ironically in response to Randy's greeting.

Her board slipped right in front of him, missing his board by less than an inch. She laughed raucously and held high a red T-shirt. "What do you think?" she asked him.

"Goes with your hair, Caramia. Try it on."

She did not slow down but pulled on the shirt as she

flew hopping down the risers. Her red gorgon's hair flowed behind her. She easily stood a head taller than Randy even off her board.

Randy stopped to pick up two cans and a bottle. He deposited them in his bulging bag, which he swung over his shoulder. He stepped back on his board to shove off.

Ahead Caramia had stopped to talk and laugh with a tween with matted hair. Across the back of Caramia's T-shirt Randy made out the words, "THE SAME TO YOU!"" Below was an enormous hand with one raised finger.

As he zipped by her, Randy whispered, "Cool shirt!"

She smiled, "Up yours too! Hey, watch out!"

Randy looked around too late and crashed into a pair of running men. He skinned both knees and felt lucky. The men rolled on the ground in pain.

Among the littered bottles and cans that had gone down with Randy were jewels and coins the like of which Randy and Caramia had never seen in the mall outside jewelry stores.

The mall policeman, who had been pursuing the two men, shook his head.

"Nice tackle, kid! Now stand back while I take care of these thieves."

The cop handcuffed both men to a bench. He got on his hands and knees to pick up the stolen jewels and coins.

"Kid, can I borrow one of your bags for their loot?"

Randy scrambled to find a bag with a solid bottom. He handed it to the officer.

Caramia asked, "Do you want us to help you search?"

"You'd better just stay clear. I don't want you to be accused of taking any of the stolen goods even accidentally."

"Those are my bottles and cans, officer," Randy exclaimed.

"Don't worry. Once I've completed my search, you can pick up whatever remains."

The officer continued picking up the loot. He kept glancing at his prisoners to be sure they were still on the bench.

The bearded jeweller who had been robbed came over and watched the officer working. He knew he could not pick up his property as the jewels and coins were now evidence. He shook his head and glared at the thieves.

When he had finished picking up the loot, the officer

took the thieves and the evidence away. The jeweller followed them.

Randy and Caramia picked up the bottles and cans and placed them back in Randy's clear bag.

Sam wandered by and spotted a gleam in the cracks of the pavement. He stooped and pulled out a stone. When he held it to the sun, the stone sparkled.

"That's a diamond!" Caramia shrieked.

Sam coolly reached in his pocket and fetched out a jeweller's loupe. He examined the stone. "It's costume jewellery made of paste."

Randy said, "Maybe you should take it to the mall police in case it's evidence."

Sam put the stone on the ground and ran his shopping cart over the stone, shattering it. "See? It's costume jewellery."

"Why do you carry that eyepiece?" Caramia asked.

Sam laughed. "Because one day I'll find a real diamond. My Dad's in the trade." Then he inched forward, scanning.

Community Service

by Susan Howe

Mourners packed the church, as expected. After all, Jim had been the town's favourite handyman for his entire working life. What Mary didn't appreciate until she stood in the porch, shaking hands as they filed past, was quite how many were women. Several of them hid red eyes and one or two still sobbed into their hankies.

Her son, handsome in his navy suit, glanced down at his mother with a small bewildered shrug. Mary smiled and patted his arm. She'd explain about Jim's 'Ladies' another time, when his grief was less new. And, if she was honest, even she was surprised by the number. So many satisfied customers!

The vicar turned from a woman he had been comforting, a puzzled frown furrowing his normally untroubled brow.

"I can't remember such a full house," he said. "I knew Jim was well regarded but this is extraordinary!"

"Yes, it's very gratifying," Mary replied.

Then, to show she was aware of the gender discrepancy, she added, "They relied on him, you know. For everything. Just like me."

Her heart swelled with affection for the man who had been her friend and lover for over forty years, with hardly a cross word in all that time. However would she —and everyone else—manage without him?

It hadn't been until after their children had grown up and moved out that the couple began to develop an expanded business plan. Despite extensive commitments in the community and a circle of good friends, they now felt they had time, energy—and love—

to spare. As the word spread, demand steadily increased.

On their rare evenings relaxing at home together they'd discuss their clients, many of them women past their prime, widows and spinsters with no one to turn to for even the most basic of maintenance work.

"So much loneliness," he'd say, with a deep sigh.

"I know, dear," she'd reply, "but you're doing your best. Maybe you should employ an assistant? You're not as young as you used to be, you know. And if you put your back out, where will that leave me?"

He would nod and promise to think about training up a successor for when he could no longer manage the long, often exhausting days, but had never quite got round to it. There was always someone urgently requiring his kindness and expertise.

And then he was gone.

Mary strolled through the sunny churchyard between her son and daughter, their arms tightly linked, and thanked God again for so many wonderful years with the most generous person she had ever known. And that he'd died in his own bed, doing what he enjoyed most.

Imagining her own funeral, whenever that might be, and the probable gender imbalance there, too, she allowed herself a private little smile.

So much love! So many satisfied customers.

Scatterlings

by Carleton Chinner

"He shouldn'a done that," says Old Henry as he picks breadcrumbs from his tangled beard. Old Henry likes to mumble.

I don't mind the mumbles. He's always been Old Henry to me. The one who found me when I had been sleeping rough for a week.

"Girl can't be sleeping in the rain," he mumbled to the world and covered my shivers with cardboard. After that I stuck around. He's always good for a smoke or a sip of goon, and he knows the best places to look for a free feed.

I know what he is on about this time. The bloke in the sharp suit. The tall, dark-haired one who likes to take a walk in the park. Old Henry don't speak about it, but sometimes he mumbles.

A hipster dude in skinny jeans walks past our bench, his barber-neat beard shining in the sun. The clothes say shabby, retro, but the beard says weekly trimming and Moroccan Oil massages.

"Spare us a smoke mate," says Old Henry, keeping his eyes low to give Skinny Jeans a chance to feel good about himself. Skinny smiles and hands him a fag, even lights it. Old Henry takes an appreciative drag and passes it to me. Smoke curls above our park bench as we watch other people with better places to go.

It's late afternoon on Tuesday. It's always Tuesday when the bloke in the suit comes. He's wearing the tired-angry smile you put on when you don't want the world to know how you feel. He walks past our bench and doesn't look at us. Just another office pony like all the others who pretend we aren't there.

"Spare us a smoke mate."

The suit sees Old Henry and the tired smile fades. He stands there, arms at his side as if he's scared they'll fly away. Old Henry gets to his feet and shambles closer to the suit, staring at him as if his tired old eyes are seeing something new. He puts a hand on the suit's shoulder.

"It's not my fault," he says.

"Get away from me you dirty dero," screams the suit in the too-high voice of a boy stuck in a man's body.

"Please," says Old Henry, his hands stretched out to beg.

The suit lashes out and hits Henry on the nose. Old Henry falls to the ground holding his bleeding nose and bawling.

"You know what that's for," says the suit as he turns and walks off to the office towers. He doesn't even look back.

I hold Old Henry until the sobbing stops. He wipes his tired eyes, and we walk to the little marble fountain where the school-kids sometimes toss in a coin when they think we're not looking. I help him wash off the blood and we sit there silent until the warmth creeps from the day.

"C'mon mate, the sun's going," he says and we walk to the warm bench on top of the hill. The one that looks out over the city. It's as cold as anywhere else, but the view feels good. Old Henry pulls the cardboard out from where he had stashed it last night and spreads it on the park bench. He lies down staring at the view.

"Night mate," he says to me then he rolls over, and above the roaring silence of the neon city I hear him whisper.

"Gawd, I hate me brother sometimes."

The Third Sphere

by Lindsey McLeod

I lay twisted on the road, left cheek squashed against the hot tarmac. I could hear blood bubbling through my nose with every wheeze. An angel stood over me, scroll in hand.

"Don't go into the light, Will. It's not your time."

I squinted up at her with my working eye. "What light?"

She looked around. "The light. Like at the end of the tunnel."

Overhead the blue sky stretched endlessly. Route 66 was not known for its tunnels. Or obstacles. It was a miracle that I had managed to crash my bike in the first place. I struggled to sit up. There was surprisingly little pain. My left arm swung uselessly, obviously broken.

She consulted the scroll. "Are you... Are you not going into the light?"

"Well you just told me not to. Which is it?"

"Definitely don't."

"Fine."

She looked perplexed. "I don't think you're supposed to be able to see me."

My bike lay several feet away. Behind it, a long smear of red coated the road. My face felt hot and sticky. I suspected I did not currently look my most dashing.

Her brown eyes were brimming with compassion. Her hair was a Hokusai painting—blonde, sculpted waves which flowed and draped around her shoulders. She was nibbling a fingernail with intense concentration, like a starving hamster. I was in love.

"Could you call me an ambulance?"

"Someone will be along shortly. I'm just here to make sure you don't go into the light."

"I think we've established that I won't."

"Right. Good."

We stared at each other.

"I'm your guardian angel," she said, a flush of embarrassment spreading across alabaster cheeks. "I'm sorry, I was only assigned to you this morning and I'm afraid I'm not very good at it. There's an admin strike going on Upstairs."

"Upstairs?"

"Upstairs," she repeated, as if that would clear things up. Her wings fluttered as she shrugged. "You know. Upstairs."

"Right. Right." I changed tack. "Can I see you again?'"

"Only when you get close to death. I mean, you shouldn't really be seeing me at all, but—"

"Then I guess I'm going to be taking up some dangerous hobbies."

"That's," she paused for a moment, looking down at me, "incredibly stupid."

"I've never been a smart man. What's good? Diving? Skiing? Mafia-related hobby?"

She gave this some thought. "Become a taxi driver."

"Huh?"

"There's all the potential danger of regular traffic accidents, plus violent passengers," she ticked these off on her fingers, "and falling asleep at the wheel is becoming a huge problem in this economy. People trying to make ends meet, you know?"

A siren wailed in the distance. "Wait, what's your name?:

She was already fading. "I'll tell you next time."

***

"How'd he take it?" the secretary asked.

"Like they all do," Lucifer said, striding into the royal quarters, "like a chump."

She tossed the scroll to a waiting minion and carelessly shrugged off her wings. They hit the floor with a feathery, muted thud.

"Tasty bait, but we could have had one of the younglings do it, you know," the secretary said, scribbling on a clipboard. "Plenty of minor demons waiting for a chance to prove themselves."

"Sometimes I feel the need to get out for a while," Lucifer said, sprawling on the vast, cast-iron throne, and kicking her heels off, "really stretch myself. Besides, Will's important. Not hugely so, in the scheme of things, but important enough. It'll be fun to break him."

***

"How'd she take it, O Lord?" the seraph asked, as I handed him the motorbike helmet.

"Like they all do," I said, "like a chump."

Coming Home

by Joy Manné

Walter scratched and scraped his key in the lock where
it rattled in his mottled, shaky hand.

"Hello, my love, my darling," he called as he pushed
open the door, forcing his quavery voice into every
corner of the large, old-fashioned apartment. He
dropped his homburg onto a shelf in the coat cupboard
and fussed his long woollen overcoat until it sat
smoothly on its varnished mahogany hanger.

"Be patient, my love. I'll be with you in a minute."

He trickled into the toilet and lowered the toilet seat
as his wife had taught him. He lathered his hands with
her lavender Marseilles soap. He looked with pale blue
eyes into the mirror as he rubbed into his thick white

hair the gel she had chosen to make it lie flat; he had to write down its name to remember it.

There was a time when drinks were waiting, when they'd walk down the corridor to the living room arm in arm, admiring the paintings they had collected over almost fifty years and hung in the stacked, abundant, old-fashioned way. He might reminisce about a good deal. She might congratulate him on a good choice.

"I'll pour drinks, my darling."

He poured a double from a bottle of Glenlivet off the mahogany drinks trolley, a wedding present fifty-one years ago. Hand quivering, ice rattling, he set his glass a silver coaster on a cherry-wood Noguchi table between facing chintz-covered armchairs. She did not like glasses to stand directly on its plate-glass surface.

"I'm sorry I'm late," He looked at her with devotion from under heavy-lidded eyes. He eased himself into his usual armchair with its back to the view of trees and sky and sipped his scotch, and sipped again, letting the amber liquid warm away the tension in his shoulders and his voice; as his eyes stared at, without seeing, a large piece of amber on a stand with a fly fossilised in its centre.

"Toby brought a new collector—modern English—to the gallery this morning. Good old Toby." Walter's smile lifted his moustaches and the corner of his eyes which sparkled. "He invited me for dinner with his family. Toby' evaluates art better than he does wine. I persuaded him to join me for lunch at the club. We ate endeavour prawns flown in this morning from Australia, and rare Angus beef, roasted as only they know how, and I had your favourite baked apple tart for dessert." Walter managed another smile, sipped again and waited for more warmth to wind through his prominent blue veins.

"We prefer to be at home together in the evening, don't we, my darling?"

He sighed, sipped, and crossed his legs the other way.

"I'd only just got back to the office before it started to rain. I couldn't get a taxi in front of the office so I took our largest umbrella and walked round the corner to Covent Garden. It was half an hour before the performance. A stream of taxis was letting people out. I nipped into one of them. "

Walter laughed with his mouth shut, making a hmmm-hmmm sound. "You were impressed the first time I showed you my little ruse." His shoulders shook with silent forced laughter.

He finished his drink.

"Susan Ryder caught you perfectly," he said. "I'm so

glad we chose her rather than Lucien Freud who would have made a monster of you, or Auerbach who would have pitted and cratered your lovely smooth skin." He pushed on armrests to help himself up. "She's caught the sparkle in your eyes, my love, my darling, and their unique colour, between blue and grey."

In small steps, he walked around the other chair until he stood in front of a portrait and kissed its lips where his mouth had left many traces before.

The Note

by John Holland

Harlan T. Spank III, aged 10, round, red-haired, putty-faced looked like a difficult child. Was a difficult child. He was cruel, selfish and argumentative, traits he inherited from his parents. His mother Marcie and his father Harlan T. Spank II had not wanted a child and tended to gratify young Harlan's wants rather than satisfy his needs. His father was a multi-millionaire property developer, although some said he had links with the underworld that went back at least one generation, and that he made his money in less than legitimate ways.

The note from the kidnappers read:

For the kid, leave $1 million in used notes in the big burnt-out oak tree by the crossroads at 2 am on

Tuesday.

At 2 am on Tuesday, the kidnappers went to the tree and found only a note from his parents. It read:

Did you mean this tree? There's another burnt-out tree just across the meadow. Which tree is it? We will pay no more than $500,000.

The next note from the kidnappers read:

Of course this tree. It's an oak. The other tree is a lime. And it's nowhere near the crossroads. $800,000 then. Put it in the burnt-out oak tree in used notes at midnight on Monday.

At midnight on Monday the kidnappers went to the tree and found only a note from his parents. It read:

Midnight is like zero hours, so did you mean midnight from Sunday going on Monday, or Monday going on Tuesday? Jeez, can't you be more exact? Also *can we change to the other tree? It's real muddy by this one. $500,000 is all we got.*

The next note from the kidnappers read:

For Christ's sake, forget the other tree. $500,000 it is then. Leave it in the burnt-out oak tree by the crossroads at fifteen minutes past midnight (00.15) on Wednesday morning the twenty seventh (27th) of March in the year 2013 (Twenty thirteen) DST (Daylight Saving Time). This is your last chance.

His parents paid up and, much to their relief, within days the kidnappers had taken young Harlan.

Sky

by Kate Murray

Darkness is all I feel at first, like a pressure on my chest making it hard to breathe and even harder to open my eyes. It doesn't shift. It is just there. I try to remember. Was I in bed?

I can't move. I remember watching a documentary once about night terrors. People sat on grey chairs in a grey room and described how they would wake and see someone near them. But they themselves would be unable to move, stuck in one position while the thing glided across the floor and reached for them. I remember not believing that it could happen to me, that I could become effectively paralysed by my own fear.

I can't move though. It could be a night terror. There could be something stalking me...

Then I hear laughter.

It isn't with me... It's an echo. Am I hearing someone from far away or is this part of my dream?

As that thought floats through my head a drop lands on my face. It is fat, cold and wet. I feel my face flinch at the impact and it acts like a switch. I can feel my face. I open my eyes. There is darkness, but not like before. Now there is a lightness of air around me. I look up and can see clouds rushing past a full moon.

I try to smile but I can't feel the muscles move in my mouth. I guess they aren't responding, which should bother me. But all I feel is calm.

"Susan?"

The cry comes from inside my head and I frown in confusion. It's like the echo. There but not there.

"Want to go out?"

I should know that voice... It should mean something to me.

Another drop hits my face and I see that there are a thousand jewels in the sky. They are hanging in the air but moving so slowly. It dawns on me that I'm seeing water drops. The dream must be working in slow motion though, because it is as if someone has hit a button on a remote. I used to do that when I watched movies, especially to look at beautiful men.

"Come on, Susan, hurry up!"

I know that voice.

A drop hits my eye and although I see it coming so slowly I can't get my eyelid closed in time. It hits with the force of a tennis ball and my eye stings as a thousand shocks go through my body. Then I see her.

Ally.

My sister.

She is smiling and holding out my jacket, the light purple one. The one we always argue whether it is lilac or purple. Purple, I think, but Ally doesn't answer.

She smiles and hands me the coat. We walk out of the door and I can see the clouds are threatening.

"Where are we going?" I ask

"There's a film I want to see."

We jump into her small fiat and are off. She drives too fast but we know the roads. We are safe, surrounded by car. Nothing can go wrong. Then we see a bird, with large black wings and a sharp beak. It tries to take off, but at the last minute Ally turns the steering wheel. We head for a hedge. The bird hits the undercarriage and is gone instantly in a haze of feathers and blood.

Someone screams. It is me.

Then I feel another drop hit my face. Does it hit my face or am I crying? I try to turn my head. I try to see Ally but I can't. All I can do is watch the jewels fall toward me in ever slowing movement. I smell petrol and a part of me wonders if I ought to move. I have seen movies where cars flip and blow up. And something like that must have happened. I'm on my back in the dirt. I can feel the gravel and mud. It's cold.

But there is no moving.

The only thing moving are the jewels, but they are so beautiful. I think I'll just watch them for a while.

"You okay, Susan?"

The voice is more than an echo but I can't even blink a reply. I'm just too tired and all I want to say is to tell them to look. It is so beautiful.

What Comes Round Goes Round

by Oonah V Joslin

"A government spokesperson has said that there is no proven link between violence as portrayed in Worldwide Corporate's latest HoloInteractives and violence on our streets. She emphasised that OldStad and other areas like it throughout the city were virtually crime-free and darned good communities in which to live." The wind-up radio wound down.

Jess struggled in on her sticks and placed three fresh eggs from the cotton bag on her arm on the rough table.

"Is that it?" asked her mother.

"Someone took one of the hens."

True—it was unusual for anyone to steal in OldStad.

Everyone was scraping by, little or no sanitation, standpipe water on the perimeter, anything they could beg, scrounge or recycle from landfill—but stealing a hen was virtually unheard of, after all—you might need a favour one day.

"Must be a stranger. Tell Dusty on your way back from milking the goat, Jess."

"Sure, Mum."

Dusty was a bully but he was the unofficial law around here and he was the nearest thing to a brick shit house they had. He made sure strangers became... familiar with the rules. Jess and Mari made sure he got some fresh milk every day and an egg if they could afford it. Many other families also contributed to his wellbeing.

Jess strung a bucket on a rope round her neck and picked up her sticks. Polio was rife in the OldStad as it was in all the satellite shanty towns. Jess considered herself lucky. She could walk. Construction for a brand new hospital was under way within sight of the perimeter but the treatment was well out of range for anybody in OldStad.

The perimeter was a recent addition, lottery and business-funded. Every five hundred yards along the high wall there was a standpipe providing clean water but it also meant the people inside were hidden from view: a convenient side effect.

Jess heard the wind-up as she approached Dusty's shack.

"A government spokesperson has said that Public Screen coverage of the 2052 Olympic Games will greatly encourage young people to take up sports as well as contributing millions to the economy and vastly improving the lives of ordinary people."

Between the lines of those two bulletins, something didn't quite add up for Jess and she wondered whether the New Stadium they were building now would end up like this old one.

"Dusty?"

He grunted a reply.

She went inside. She poured some milk from the bucket into a tall jug on the table. She placed her sticks by the wall.

"No eggs today?"

"Mother said to tell you there's a stranger about— one of the chickens is missing," she said, undoing her blouse.

Biographies

Carleton Chinner is an Australian born writer who spent his childhood in apartheid South Africa and left with a wealth of stories to tell. He has survived a gun fight, discovered dead bodies and dived with sharks. When not writing, he works as a project manager on large government programs.

Annie Evett is a prolific scribbler of characters, weaver of storylines, champion of the short story, professional cat herder, wielder of a balanced editing razor while beating  recalcitrant words into shape. She is a contributing editor in a number of publications and manages a small indie publishing house committed to promoting the short story form. She tweets @AnnieEvett, is Linkedin and can be stalked on http://annieevett.com

 **E. W. Farnsworth** has won numerous writing prizes over the last three years. He lives and writes in Arizona, USA. For more information, please see ewfarnsworth.com.

Originally **Alyson Faye** was a teacher/tutor who wrote children's books/poetry as a hobby. Fast forward to 2016 where she lives near Bronte terrain in Yorkshire. Alyson writes noir Flash Fiction and spooky tales, lives with her family and 3 cats, is a confirmed chocoholic; and still hopeless at maths. Find more on www.alysonfayewordpress.wordpress.com

Epiphany Ferrell's writing career includes gigs at a coonhound magazine, a couple of newspapers and a university communications team. Her stories appear in *The Potamac, Clamor 2015, Cooper Street, PaperTape Magazine, Prairie Wolf Press Review, DarkFire, Seven Hills Review, Helix Literary Magazine* and other places. She is a fiction editor for Mojave River Review. She makes her home with dogs, cats, chickens and horses -- and a couple of important people -- at Resurrection Mule Farm in Southern Illinois.

Emily Forster is a bored archaeologist and aspiring novelist. Living in Yorkshire (UK) she loves the outdoors and has a substantial collection of waterproof clothing.

Paul Alex Gray enjoys writing speculative fiction that cuts a jagged line to a magical real world. His work has been published in *Ad Hoc Fiction, 365 Tomorrows* and *101 Words*. Growing up in Australia, Paul traveled the world and now lives in Canada with his wife and two children.

Keith Gillison is a UK writer of flash fiction, short stories and novels in many genres including humour and crime. His stories have been published in magazines, anthologies and online. His first novel, *The Boss Killers*, is a dark humour crime novel and was self-published in 2015. Follow Keith on www.facebook.com/keithgillisonauthor/

John Holland is an award-winning short fiction writer from Gloucestershire in the UK. He also runs the twice yearly Stroud Short Stories event.

Jodie How lives in Busselton, WA. She runs two writers groups and helps to organise author visits and local bookish events. She has been writing part-time for about four years. Her favourite stories are ones that keep her guessing, with a psychological twist or two.

Susan Howe's stories and flash fictions have been published and placed in competitions many times. A proud but displaced Yorkshirewoman, brevity is in her DNA.

Oonah V Joslin's stories and poems have been published online and in various print anthologies. Her novella *A Genie in a Jam*, is serialised at *Bewildering Stories*. She is poetry editor at *Linnets Wings. Three pound of cells* is available at https://www.createspace.com/6617022. Follow Oonah on Facebook or Parallel Oonaverse.

Heather Harris McFarlane lives and works near Seattle, WA, where she runs an independent and inclusive comic shop and participates in panel discussions at  comics industry conventions. Her top priority when it comes to fiction - writing it and selling it - is to provide stories that are as diverse as those who need it. Fiction is the lens through which we make sense of a world we can't always understand.

Lindsey McLeod is an Executive Assistant from Edinburgh. She has published several short stories through 365 Tomorrows. She is currently working on two novels and a creative writing degree, as well as a way to fit more hours into a day.

Joy Manné would prefer to let her stories speak for

themselves as she never knows what to say about herself. In a former life she explored what it  means to be human through Conscious Breathing Techniques, Family Constellations and Story. Now she writes fiction. Find more about her on http://www.joymanne.org/

A Mitchell wields a mean 6 HB pencil infusing her eclectic artwork with years of teaching, traversing the corporate landscape and motherhood.

An emerging artist and photographer, she has had a number of prints, brush painting and sketches published. Follow her on Facebook https://www.facebook.com/AMitchellArtist

Kate Murray

has recently completed her Masters in Creative Writing. She is currently working on her third short story anthology and had had a number of short stories accepted in magazines and ebook anthologies, such as *The Lampeter Review* and the *What the Dickens* anthology *Busker*. More about Kate on https://kateomurray.com

Sylvia Petter is an Australian based in Vienna who writes short, long, serious and fun. She has a PhD in Creative Writing and has published the collections, *The Past Present (2001), Back Burning (2007), Mercury Blobs (2013)*, and writing as AstridL, *Consuming the Muse – erotic tales (2013)*.

A German translation of several of her stories was published in 2014 as *Geflimmer der Vergangenheit*.

More at her website, www.sylviapetter.com .

Margie Riley's been a bibliophile forever and knows that writing is a complicated game. Published in Ether Books,  *Stringybark's Behind the Wattles* , *No Tea Tomorrow*, and the national newspaper, *The Australian.* She's contributed to various online writers' mags and is an inveterate commentator. She belongs to a book club (doesn't everybody?) and a writers' group. She uses her status as an elder to justify her gentle wielding of the editor's red pen. Caducity hasn't quite set in—yet. She can be found here www.bettermanuscriptediting.com.au, and on Facebook.

Author

Catherine Russell shares her life with her high school sweetheart, their son, and other ferocious creatures in the Wilds of Ohio while writing short stories, composing poetry, and learning more about the craft every day. Her work has been published in *Flash Me* magazine, *Metro Fiction*, *Beyond Centauri*, and the '*Best of Friday Flash – Volume One*' and '*-Volume Two*' anthologies, as well as *Poetry Quarterly* and *Three Line Poetry*. She can be found https://catherinerussellwriter.wordpress.com

Christopher Stanley

lives on a hill in England with his three sons who share a birthday but aren't triplets. In 2016, his stories won multiple prizes, as well as being published in places like The *Molotov Cocktail*, *Jellyfish Review*, *The Short Story*, and in the *National Flash Fiction Day* anthology. He visits the family bungalow in Eccles-on-Sea a few times a year, often travelling up at night with his eldest son. Find out more about his writing in his blog http://whenonlywordsareleft.wordpress.com and follow him on Twitter @allthosestrings

Jon Stubbington

lives and writes on the edge of a moor in Devon, England. This is not as poetic as it sounds. His writing has been published in magazines, performed in pubs, and broadcast on radio in Ireland. You can also find him at recycledwords.co.uk or on twitter @recycled_words.

About the Publisher

Raging Aardvark Publications is an Australian indie publisher which promotes creative artists of edgy, off-kilter work in anthologies of short stories, flash fiction and poetry, as well as delving into non-fiction.

They are committed to sourcing a wide range of cross-genre fiction which not only pushes boundaries, but also stirs the emotions of readers.

Non-fiction themes explore living an authentic life, balancing the challenges of the 21st Century and exploring the vast range of experiences within relationships.

Raging Aardvark supports International Flash Fiction Day through an extensive competition culminating in the anthology *Twisted Tales*.

As their literary imprint, *Cats With Thumbs*, they produce a blogzine biannually with a collected anthology of favourite poetry, short stories, artwork and photography; published in July.

Titles available from Amazon include:

Choose your Adventures—written by a number of authors

History's Keeper

Dust and Death

Zombie Now

Anthologies involving a number of authors

New Sun Rising—Stories for Japan

Twisted Tales 2012—Flash Fiction with a Twist

Twisted Tales 2013—Flash Fiction with a Twist

Twisted Tales 2014—Flash Fiction with a Twist

Twisted Tales 2015—Flash Fiction with a Twist

Cats With Thumbs 2016

Single author anthologies

Consuming the Muse—erotic tales—AstridL

Mercury Blobs—Sylvia Petter

Love Just Is—Kate Murray

Shadows Close—Kate Murray

Sandman—Simon Humphreys

Non Fiction

Reclaim—Sex after Birth—Annie Evett

It's up to Me—Warren Hooke

Upcoming Titles

Raunchy Recipes—Erotic tales blended with luscious recipes

Sartres' Lonely Toybox—Annie Evett

Brother Dragon and Racoon walk the Camino - Annie Evett

Letters to Saffy—Kiki Jarrott

For more information, check their website.

http://ragingaardvark.com

www.ingramcontent.com/pod-product-compliance
Lightning Source LLC
Chambersburg PA
CBHW060627130626
46555CB00002B/695